*Sarah Simpson's*
*Rules for Living*

# Sarah Simpson's
# Rules * for * Living

## REBECCA RUPP

CANDLEWICK PRESS
CAMBRIDGE, MASSACHUSETTS

Copyright © 2008 by Rebecca Rupp

First edition 2008

Library of Congress Cataloging-in-Publication Data is available.

Library of Congress Catalog Number pending

ISBN 978-0-7636-3220-5

2 4 6 8 10 9 7 5 3 1

Printed in the United States of America

This book was typeset in Veljovic.

Candlewick Press
2067 Massachusetts Avenue
Cambridge, Massachusetts 02140

visit us at www.candlewick.com

*For Molly*

## SARAH SIMPSON'S RULES FOR LIVING

1. Don't lie.

2. Don't trust anybody but cats.

3. Don't expect happy endings.

4. Drink skim milk.

5. Avoid blondes.

JANUARY 1

It is New Year's Day, and I have decided to keep a
journal. Sally, my mother, says this is a good idea because I got a journal for Christmas from my aunt
Kate and if I don't write in it, what else am I going to
do with it?

"You can keep your lists in it," Andrea said.

Andrea is Sally's best friend, and she does not
approve of lists. There are two kinds of people in the
world, says Andrea: the list makers and the free spirits.
Andrea is a free spirit. She has lots of frizzy hair in
dreadlocks, and she wears big clanky jewelry and
clothes in loud patterns that are not flattering to
her hips. Andrea teaches Women's Studies and Gen-
der and Social Issues at Pelham State College, right
across the hall from where Sally teaches English
literature.

People who make lists, says Andrea, are putting
all their time in boxes and not leaving themselves
open to new experiences like suddenly buying a parrot
or going to Italy for the weekend.

But I think lists are a way of putting your thoughts
in order. Also I think it is important to plan.

REASONS WHY ANDREA SHOULD MAKE LISTS

1. She is always forgetting her appointments with her therapist.
2. Whenever she promises to bring something over for dessert, she ends up leaving it at home in her refrigerator.

So then Sally said that people often start journals by introducing themselves. So that is what I am going to do.

My name is Sarah Elizabeth Simpson. I am twelve years old. I have orange hair and I am fat.

Sally says it's baby fat, but that sounds like crap to me. Emily Harris, who is blond and thin and the most popular girl in my class, does not have baby fat.

Sally and I live in Pelham, Vermont, at the very edge of town, where the sidewalk ends and the woods begin. We have two cats, named Virginia Woolf and Samuel Johnson, though we mostly call them Ginger and Sam. Ginger is almost as old as I am, but Sam is just a kitten. He is a replacement for Charles Dickens, who vanished last year under mysterious circumstances. We suspect Mr. Binns, an unfriendly neighbor who has scrubby little chickens and a shotgun.

My father does not live with us anymore. He lives in Los Angeles, California, with his new wife, who is a tennis instructor named Kim.

THINGS I DO NOT LIKE ABOUT KIM
1. She wears a Wonderbra.
2. She has long blond hair that she's always flinging around to make sure that everybody notices that she has long blond hair.
3. She is boring to talk to.
4. She giggles through her nose.

Kim looks exactly like a Barbie doll. Andrea, when I'm not supposed to be listening, refers to Kim and my father as Barbie and Ken and asks how life is going at Barbie's Malibu Beach House. Actually my father and Kim do not have a beach house. They live in a development about five minutes from the beach. I saw a picture of it. All the houses are painted pink and pale blue and lime green and look like brand-new candy boxes.

Our house is old and white and peely, and part of the back porch is falling down.

My mother has a boyfriend named Jonah. She doesn't call him her boyfriend. She says he's just a good friend. But I can see the handwriting on the wall. He's here practically all the time, with his little boy, whose name is George. I think that's a stodgy name for a little kid. If I had a little boy, I'd name him Vladimir.

George has shaggy brown hair, and he's always dragging this ratty stuffed bear around.

THINGS I DO NOT LIKE ABOUT JONAH
1. He always sits in the cats' chair.
2. He is not nearly as good-looking as my father. He is going bald on top, and he has a potbelly.
3. He drives a horrible old blue van with bumper stickers all over it that say things like SAVE THE WHALES and VISUALIZE WHIRLED PEAS.
4. He sings stupid songs.
5. He has a beard.

**Later**

It is New Year's Day night. I am the only one awake. Sally and the cats are asleep. George and Jonah have gone home.

George and Jonah were here for dinner, which was pot roast and potato pancakes. Most people have ham at New Year's, but we don't because I won't eat pigs because of Piglet. Piglet is my favorite *Pooh* character. Jonah eats pigs, but not around me.

Jonah brought a bottle of champagne for him and Sally and a bottle of sparkling cider for me and George. Then he proposed toasts.

THINGS WE TOASTED
1. Good friends.
2. The future.
3. The Revolution.
4. Bears.

"What Revolution?" I said, and Jonah said that the Revolution is when the good people take over the world and everybody uses solar power and eats organic vegetables.

After dinner we went for a walk in the snow. The snow was coming down in fat fluffy flakes like the snow in a snow globe. If you looked straight up into the snow, you could imagine that everything was upside down and you were falling into the sky.

George went running ahead with his bear and his stupid floppy boots, trying to catch snowflakes on his tongue, and Jonah took Sally's hand and tucked it through his arm. Sally can say he's just a friend all she wants, but I know better.

Then they started talking about their New Year's resolutions. Sally's is the same every year: "Simplify, simplify." That's a quote from Henry David Thoreau. Sally thinks that life is too cluttered and needs to be pared down. I can think of things to pare down too, but mine are not the same as Sally's.

George's resolution is to grow enough so that he can ride the Mountain of Death roller coaster next summer at the Pelham Fair. Short little kids are not allowed on the Mountain of Death roller coaster. George is five and small for his age. Jonah asked me what my resolutions were and I said I didn't know.

Jonah has not made any resolutions yet either, but I could think of some.

RESOLUTIONS FOR JONAH

1. Lose 25 pounds.
2. Sell the van.
3. Throw out that shirt with the sea horses on it.
4. Quit singing "We Shall Overcome."
5. Shave.

I just looked up *resolution* in the dictionary that I got for Christmas from my aunt Elaine. Aunt Elaine always gives improving presents, like wool socks and yoga mats.

> *resolution* (n.) 1. A resolute temper; boldness and firmness of purpose. 2. An intention.

MY RESOLUTIONS FOR THE NEW YEAR

1. Get rid of Kim.
2. Get rid of Jonah.
3. Dye my hair.
4. Change my name and move to Australia.

## JANUARY 2
### Just barely

It is almost one o'clock in the morning, but I can't get to sleep. Thoughts keep going around in my head.

New Year's Day is the anniversary of the day my whole life changed. Last year this was the day my father left. Before he went, we had a talk and he told me all about how married people sometimes grow in different directions and about meeting Kim and realizing that she was his soul mate and how the new year is a time for new beginnings.

"A new beginning for all of us, pumpkin," he said. But I don't see how it was a new beginning for Sally and me. I think if he really loved me, he would have stayed home.

Also I hate it when he calls me pumpkin.

Andrea says that Kim is a calculating bimbo, but Sally says no and that anyway the divorce was her fault too, because she and my father got married too young and they turned out not to have much in common, except me.

I don't see that Sally has much in common with Jonah either.

Sally rides a bicycle and likes classical music. Jonah just sits. He likes sappy folk songs.

Last year at this time everything was normal and now everything has fallen apart. I read once that the universe started with an explosion and that ever since all the stars and galaxies have been speeding off into space, moving away from each other as fast as they can. Nobody knows whether the stars will keep moving away from each other forever or whether someday they'll all start moving backward and come back together again.

In my opinion, once something falls apart, it never comes back together again. I bet the stars are going to keep moving away from each other forever.

MY LIST OF AWFUL THINGS
1. The universe is falling apart.
2. The good people will never take over the world.
3. Grown-ups lie.
4. I am really ugly.

5. If any boy ever likes me, it will be that geek
   Horace Zimmerman.

It's still snowing. I feel like I'm falling upside down into the sky.

## JANUARY 6

I am going to be in a play at school.

My school is called Pelham Free Academy. That sounds fancy, but it's really just a dumpy school made out of cement blocks painted a sort of yellowy color with a chain-link fence around it. The sixth-grade teacher is named Winona Bentley. Every time we have a school vacation, Ms. Bentley goes to workshops and conferences and comes back with new ideas for improving our minds. Over Christmas, she spent two days in Boston learning about Teaching Literature through Dramatic Arts in the Classroom.

So now we're doing this play.

The play is all about the Greek myths. Emily Harris is Aphrodite. Ronnie Pincus, who has biceps from working weekends and summers on his family's farm, is Zeus. Horace Zimmerman, who is tall and skinny and wears thick black glasses, is Hades.

I am Persephone, the brainless drip who ate the pomegranate seeds and ended up spending half her life in hell.

THINGS I HATE ABOUT THIS PLAY

1. Getting up in front of people.
2. Being dragged into the Underworld by Horace Zimmerman.
3. Wearing toilet-paper flowers in my hair.
4. Not knowing what a pomegranate is.

## JANUARY 7

From Aunt Elaine's dictionary:

> *pomegranate* (n.) From the Old French *pome grenate,* many-seeded apple. A fruit with a tough skin containing many seeds in a red pulp. The tree bearing this fruit, *Punica granatum,* is native to N. Africa and W. Asia.

At the new year in Greece, Sally says, people throw a pomegranate on the floor. If it smashes into lots of little pieces, that means good luck. We should have done that, she said.

I think it's a good thing we didn't. It would have been too depressing.

It probably would have bounced.

George thinks Persephone is a great part, even with the toilet paper. He has been in two plays in kindergarten. In one of them he played the letter B, and in the other he was a toadstool. Jonah says he was particularly good at the toadstool because it is difficult to play a fungus with distinction.

It must be nice to be five.

George has a picture book of the myth of Persephone from the library and he made me read it to him twice while Sally and Jonah were out in the kitchen, giggling and doing the dishes. It begins with Demeter, goddess of the harvest, and her daughter, Persephone, picking daisies in a meadow. Demeter is fat and pink and cheerful-looking and has a basket full of fruit and stuff. Persephone is blond and looks like Emily Harris.

Then Persephone wanders out of her mother's sight and the minute she does, Hades, looking a bit like Elvis Presley, pops out of the ground in a black chariot pulled by big black horses and he grabs her and gallops off with her to the Underworld, which is dark and gloomy and looks like a basement. Persephone hates it there, even though Hades loads her with jewelry and makes her his queen. Above-ground, Demeter is miserable too. She loses weight, her hair turns gray, and she cries all the time and forgets about the harvest, so everybody in the world is starving and it's always winter.

Finally they strike a deal: Persephone can go back home, provided she hasn't eaten any of the Underworld food. But it turns out she's nibbled these pomegranate seeds. So she can only go home for half the year. The rest of the time she has to spend with Hades.

The last page of the book shows Persephone running out of a cave laughing, and her mother is laughing, and everything is sunshine and lambs. George loves that. He doesn't seem to worry about the fact that in just a little while she'll be headed right back down to hell again.

George's mother is dead. She was killed in a car crash when George was two.

George thinks she's been turned into a star. She's up in the sky, he thinks, twinkling at him.

GOOD THINGS ABOUT BEING FIVE

1. You're still cute.
2. You can drag a bear around.
3. You don't worry about anything.
4. You don't think bad things can happen.
5. You don't understand what it means to
   be dead.

BAD THINGS ABOUT BEING FIVE

1. You're too short to ride the roller coaster.
2. You have to go to bed at seven o'clock.
3. People lie to you.

## JANUARY 20

A Christmas package just arrived from my father and Kim. It's late because they weren't around for the holidays. They were skiing in Austria. They sent a picture that shows them standing in front of a ski chalet with their arms around each other, wearing goggles and forest-green ski suits and clunky boots that look like the sort of boots the astronauts wore on the moon. They're both very tan, and Kim is wearing purple lipstick.

WHAT I GOT FROM MY FATHER AND KIM FOR CHRISTMAS
1. A T-shirt with a sequin picture of a unicorn on it.
2. A CD by a group called the Duck Monkeys.
3. Blue fingernail polish.
4. A gold ankle bracelet.
5. A coupon for membership in a health club.

WHAT MY FATHER AND KIM KNOW ABOUT ME
1. Nothing.

If Elvis Presley dragged me off to the Underworld, nobody would care. My father has Kim. Sally would miss me for a while, but now she has Jonah and George. Even Ginger and Sam only like me because I let them sleep on my pillow.

I told Sally this and she said not to be ridiculous. She said she would be very jealous if I were kidnapped by Elvis Presley.

Then she borrowed the Duck Monkeys.

Last year today was Purple Feathered Hat Day. It was Sally's and my private and personal holiday.

Sally started it because I hated going to school because nobody liked me there and last year it was a lot worse because everybody was talking behind my back about my father and Kim. That's the worst part of living in a small town. There's no privacy. Everybody always knows everything about everybody else, like who's got false teeth and who doesn't pay their bills and who backed their car into the streetlight pole on Second Street and who left all those beer bottles in the park and who just moved to California with a giggly blond tennis player who has boobs the size of cantaloupes. I don't know which was worse, the kids who were mean about it or the teachers who were sympathetic and wanted to know how I was doing, dear. Anyway, I was feeling really bad, so Sally started Purple Feathered Hat Day.

We went to Burlington, just the two of us, and we bought these crazy purple hats covered with sequins and glitter and feathers in a gift shop—the silly kind of gift shop that sells stuff like earrings shaped like lizards and Mexican jumping beans and puddles of ink made out of plastic. Then we put them on and we went to a fancy restaurant for lunch where we had all the courses—appetizers and soups and entrées, and then chocolate cheesecake for dessert—and Sally let me have sips of wine from her glass when the waiter wasn't looking. The waiter was named Bernard and he had a curly mustache.

Then we went to the bookstore because Sally says that no one can be totally miserable when they're reading a really good book, so we bought some, and then we sang songs in the car all the way home.

This year Sally didn't even remember about Purple Feathered Hat Day.

Anyway she doesn't have time anymore.

She's always busy doing something with Jonah.

The only person at school who is weirder than I am is Horace Zimmerman. Horace's father teaches Latin at a private boys' school over in New York, and his mother works at an art gallery in Burlington. They are both tall and skinny and whispery, like a pair of very well-educated giraffes.

Horace is tall and skinny too, but not whispery at all. Horace is a political activist. He believes in causes. He is always putting up signs or asking people to sign petitions or having loud terrible arguments over the nature of justice or the dangers of global warming or the solution to world hunger. He once got sent to the principal's office for getting in a fight with Jason Dobbs about the spotted owl. And last semester he lay down in front of a bulldozer to protest filling in the wetlands to make a parking lot for the new supermarket, but that didn't work out very well because it was the wrong bulldozer.

Horace thinks that if people try hard enough, they can make a difference, but I think Horace is full of crap. I think things just happen to you and then you're stuck with them. Like Kim.

BAD THINGS ABOUT HORACE

1. He has a stupid name.
2. He looks geeky.
3. He acts geeky.
4. He wears really thick glasses.
5. He argues with everybody all the time.
6. He is always trying to make people sign petitions.
7. He has this really dippy glow-in-the-dark Alternative Energy baseball cap.

GOOD THINGS ABOUT HORACE

1. He is very smart.

Horace and I have a lot of time to talk at rehearsals because we are the only god and goddess in the play who know their lines. So far we have discussed world hunger, the destruction of mountain habitats, and tattoos. Emily Harris has a butterfly tattoo on her ankle. Sally won't let me get a tattoo. She says you shouldn't do anything to your body that you wouldn't want to show to a board of directors when you're 38, divorced, and applying for a job.

Horace says Andrea is wrong about lists. A list, says Horace, is a first step toward attaining one's life goals. Horace can sometimes be very pompous.

LISTS KEPT BY HORACE
1. Things He Plans to Accomplish in the Course of His Life
2. Places He Plans to Visit Before He Dies
3. World Problems That Need to Be Solved

He is going to check these off as he accomplishes, visits, or solves them.

NUMBER OF THINGS CHECKED OFF BY HORACE SO FAR
1. 0

In English class today, our vocabulary word for the day was *pulchritude.* Ronnie Pincus thought it had something to do with chickens, but it does not.

> *pulchritude* (n.) Physical beauty;
> comeliness.

Pulchritude is something that I do not have. Emily Harris does. She looks good even in a pillowcase. That's what we're all wearing for the play. Tunics made out of pillowcases. In her pillowcase, Emily looks like a fashion model. She has this very tiny waist, like Scarlett O'Hara in *Gone with the Wind.* I have no waist at all. In my pillowcase, I look like an orange cow that got tangled in a roll of toilet paper.

All through rehearsal today, I kept thinking about *Anne of Green Gables,* which is one of my favorite books. I love Anne because she uses her imagination all the time and because she has awful orange hair too. There's a part in the book where Anne tries to decide which she would rather be:

divinely beautiful or dazzlingly clever or angelically good. Anne could never make up her mind. But I know which one I'd be. I'd be divinely beautiful.

Sally says it's what you are, not what you look like, that's important, but that's the sort of thing mothers say when they're trying to make you feel better. If Sally really thinks that, she's totally whacked.

If you're beautiful enough, you can always get what you want.

Look at Kim.

Horace Zimmerman looks even worse than I do in a pillowcase. It makes him look like a marshmallow on stilts.

FEBRUARY 7

Emily Harris is the captain of the Pelham Prancers. That is the girls' field hockey team. All the field hockey players wear white T-shirts and little maroon plaid pleated skirts and maroon kneesocks. Emily Harris looks so good in that little pleated skirt that she once made some high-school boys in a pickup truck drive into a ditch.

It is a good thing that I don't play field hockey because I know what I would look like in that pleated skirt.

I would look like an orange cow.

Horace says wanting to be divinely beautiful is an unworthy ambition. He thinks everybody should try to be angelically good. Then people would be nicer to each other, and the world would be a better place.

Also Horace says there's nothing wrong with orange hair. Lots of famous people have had orange hair. Like Thomas Jefferson and Queen Elizabeth I.

REASONS WHY HORACE KNOWS NOTHING ABOUT THIS
1. He is always buttoning his shirts crooked.

FEBRUARY 14

I hate Valentine's Day. It's nice for the people who are running around being in love, but a lot of people aren't, and how do you think it makes them feel?

It makes them feel lousy.

WHAT I GOT FOR VALENTINE'S DAY
1. Nothing.

WHAT EMILY HARRIS GOT FOR VALENTINE'S DAY
1. Two boxes of chocolates.
2. Eleven cards.
3. A red rose from Dylan Guthrie, who goes to the high school.

Last year on Valentine's Day, which was after my father left but before Sally met Jonah, Andrea came over and we had pizza and then Sally and Andrea watched *Alien* because Sally said she wanted to watch a movie in which everybody dies except the woman and the cat.

This year Jonah and George came over with a sort of pizza they'd made themselves that was supposed to be shaped like a heart but actually looked like a giant tadpole with cheese. Jonah brought a box of chocolates for everybody and a big bouquet of roses for Sally and then we watched *The Goodbye Girl,* in which Marsha Mason has been dumped by every man she's ever known until she and her adorable little daughter meet Richard Dreyfuss, who is kind and funny and truly loves her. By the time we got to the happy ending, I was wishing for an acid-dripping monster to leap out from under the bed.

George brought his valentines over to show me. He got seventeen because that's how many other kids there are in his class and his teacher insists that everyone be fair. I think that is a huge mistake. Love isn't fair. They might as well learn that now.

Jonah's dead wife was named Jenny. I heard all about her one day last fall when I was sitting on the stairs reading a library book and Jonah was talking to Sally in the living room.

Her car got hit by a truck when she was on her way home from work. There was freezing rain, and this huge truck just skidded across the road and smashed into her. She was dead by the time they got her to the hospital. Jonah said his whole life changed then, just in a few seconds. He said he wanted to die too. He said he might have if it hadn't been for George.

I knew what he meant about your whole life changing just in a few seconds.

Last year on New Year's Day, when my father said good-bye, everything turned upside down forever. It was as if there was one life before the good-bye and another life after it, and once you moved into the after-good-bye life, you couldn't ever get back, no matter how hard you tried.

Ryan Matthews, whose mother is a physicist, says that every time someone makes a decision, everything splits into parallel universes. There's a universe in which my father left and a universe in which he decided not to. There's a universe in which Jenny got hit by the truck and one in which the truck missed her.

What I don't understand is why I have to be stuck in this universe. I'd rather be in the other one, the one without Kim.

I guess it isn't fair to say my whole life changed in seconds. I already knew what my father was going to say. I mean he was packing and everything.

Today I got a letter from my father. It's written on stationery from the Sun Valley Inn and Recreation Lodge, with Jacuzzis in the Rooms. There is a picture of one of the rooms at the top of the page. It has a round bed with an orange bedspread, a big pot of ferns, and a view of mountains. You can just see the Jacuzzi through the open bathroom door, with a lot of fluffy towels piled up next to it and a guest sitting in it. The guest has a sort of boiled-lobster expression and is not a very good advertisement for the Sun Valley Inn.

WHAT MY FATHER SAID
1. He and Kim are having a wonderful time.
2. This summer, if I come for a visit, Kim will teach me how to surf.
3. He heard from Sally that I am still upset about the divorce.
4. He is sorry that I am feeling bad.
5. He hopes that someday when I'm older, I'll understand why he had to leave.

At the bottom of the page, Kim wrote, "Love from Kim" in pink ink.

I don't see why Sally had to go and tell him that about being upset about the divorce. Besides, how does Sally know whether I'm upset or not?

OTHER THINGS I DO NOT UNDERSTAND
1. What's so great about being boiled in a Jacuzzi.
2. How you know which end to put the pillows on a round bed.
3. What my father sees in Kim.

I'll bet she only wants to teach me how to surf because she hopes I'll get eaten by a shark.

## MARCH 2

In history class we are reading "Excerpts from *The Autobiography of Benjamin Franklin.*" Benjamin Franklin was a list maker. He once made this list of the things you have to do to become a morally perfect person. Then he would keep track of how he did every day by checking things off in a little notebook.

BENJAMIN FRANKLIN'S RULES FOR LIVING
1. Don't eat or drink too much.
2. Don't talk all the time and especially don't gossip.
3. Be neat.
4. Do everything you've promised to do.
5. Be thrifty.
6. Work hard.
7. Don't lie.
8. Don't hurt other people.
9. Don't get mad.
10. Take baths.
11. Don't sweat the small stuff.
12. Don't sleep around.
13. Act like Jesus and Socrates.

WAYS IN WHICH THE PEOPLE I KNOW ARE NOT
MORALLY PERFECT

1. Sally: 3, 4, 7, 8, 11, 13.
2. My father: 4, 5, 6, 7, 8, 12, 13.
3. Kim: 2, 5, 6, 7, 8, 12, 13.
4. Jonah: 1, 3, 7, 13.
5. Horace: 2, 3, 9.

I am giving Horace the benefit of the doubt on 13 '
because, just like Socrates, he goes around asking
really annoying questions all the time.

Jason Dobbs says that Horace is a jerk.

Horace is in trouble for taking a stand against world hunger. He took this stand at lunchtime in the cafeteria next to the trash bins.

Horace says that every five seconds a little kid in Africa dies of starvation. Horace thinks we should be doing something about it. At the very least, says Horace, we shouldn't be wasting food. A village in Africa could live for a month, says Horace, on the food our school throws away. So he stood by the trash bins and yelled at people. Horace calls this raising consciousness.

WHAT PEOPLE SAID ABOUT THIS
1. Ryan Matthews said he was throwing out his sloppy joe because it looked and tasted like dog poo, and if the starving kids in Africa want it, they can have it.
2. Ronnie Pincus said he was throwing his sandwich away because by now his mother ought to know that he hates tuna fish.
3. Katie Costello said she was just recycling her yogurt container, so please stop yelling in

her ear because she has three-year-old twin
sisters and she hears enough yelling at home.

4. Emily Harris said please shut up.

5. Jason Dobbs said shut up without the please.

Then Mr. Fitzpatrick, who was the lunch monitor
and who has one deaf ear from an accident with an
outboard motor, finally noticed Horace and made
Horace go to the principal's office.

MARCH 7

The principal was very nice, Horace said. She sympathizes with his ideals. But she told him to stop the yelling. Yelling is not consciousness raising, she said. It is harassment. Besides it is bad for the vocal cords. Also if you are going to make stands, there are more effective places to make them than next to the cafeteria trash bins.

The principal's name is Gloria Alice Zebrowski. She is short and round and has grayish hair in tight little curls all over her head. When she was a little girl, she had long chestnut-brown ringlets. Ms. Zebrowski comes from New York City and grew up in an apartment building not far from Central Park. But she prefers living in Pelham, except that there's nowhere to buy good bagels.

I know all this because the year before my father left I spent a lot of time in her office because my grades were dropping and I was exhibiting antisocial behavior and Ms. Zebrowski would talk to me and then she would ask if I needed any help and if something was wrong at home.

I always said no.

Then Ms. Zebrowski would say that overcoming difficulties is what makes people stronger and that it's important to hope for the best because then the best has a way of happening.

I don't think that no was exactly a lie. I think I was trying to make myself believe that there really wasn't anything wrong. But I must have known deep down, because Sally and my father weren't talking to each other much and my father was going off on all these "business trips."

That's how Andrea said it, making her fingers go like quotation marks.

The wife is always the last to know, Andrea said.

Andrea doesn't know what she's talking about. Sally knew what was going on. She just didn't tell me.

The last to know is the kid.

MARCH 10

ANNOYING QUESTIONS ASKED TODAY BY
HORACE
1. If you could create world peace by pressing a
   button and killing just one person, would you
   do it?
2. If atoms are mostly space, how come we can't
   walk through walls?
3. How do you know the world is real and not
   just some enormous virtual-reality game
   being played by superior alien beings?
4. Did you ever think that people would like
   you a lot better if you didn't look so cross all
   the time?

ANSWERS TO ANNOYING QUESTIONS ASKED
TODAY BY HORACE
1. Jason Dobbs said he wouldn't do it because
   who wants world peace anyway. Jason's older
   brother Preston is in the Marines. Katie
   Costello said she would do it, depending on
   who the person was. Maybe it would be some

very old, mean person that nobody likes and who hardly had any more time to live anyway. "But what if it was somebody you really loved, like your father or mother?" Emily Harris said. "What if it was Kim?" I said.

2. Ryan Matthews said that in theory we *can* walk through walls but that statistically it is very, very unlikely, and he should know because his mother is a physicist . A lot of the boys tried it and didn't make it, which was too bad because I thought it would be sort of fun if Jason Dobbs got stuck halfway.

3. Emily Harris said that the world being a virtual-reality game thing was stupid because if everything was a virtual-reality game, we'd all just be puppets and wouldn't be able to think for ourselves. It doesn't seem stupid to me. Except that I don't think we live in a game being played by superior alien beings. I think we live in a game being played by some dumb sadistic alien teenager. The kind of creep who kicks anthills just to

watch all the ants scuttle around and
freak out.

4. I asked Sally if I looked cross all the time and
she said that it would be nice if I showed my
beautiful smile more, which is the same thing
as saying yes.

MARCH 13

Friday the 13th

A Very Unlucky Day

Today at school we talked about superstitions. Superstitions, says Ms. Bentley, are irrational beliefs. Reading your horoscope is a superstition. So is thinking that four-leaf clovers are lucky or worrying about black cats crossing your path or refusing to sit down if you're the thirteenth person at the dinner table. This was our vocabulary word for the day:

> *triskaidekaphobia* (n.) Fear of the
> number 13.

Triskaidekaphobia, says Ms. Bentley, is a superstition. Friday the 13th is no luckier or unluckier than any other day.

THINGS THAT HAPPENED TODAY, FRIDAY THE 13TH

1. Emily Harris had a premonition of disaster. Then she twisted her ankle getting off the school bus.

2. Ryan Matthews forgot his math homework.

3. Jason Dobbs lost his hand-stitched artificial leather wallet, which contained two dollar bills, five collectible baseball cards, and a photograph of his dead cocker spaniel.

4. Ronnie Pincus stepped on an egg.

5. Katie Costello was bitten by a hamster.

6. Horace's fountain pen leaked all over his pants.

Three months from today is my birthday. I was born on Friday the 13$^{th}$. Sally says that goes to show that 13 is really the luckiest number there is, but history is not on her side.

Just because something is irrational doesn't mean it isn't real.

**MARCH 16**

Today we discussed puberty in health class.

Emily Harris is looking forward to puberty. I am not.

BAD THINGS ABOUT GETTING OLDER
1. More responsibility.
2. Algebra.
3. Embarrassing zits.
4. Embarrassing underwear.
5. Embarrassing school dances.
6. Having to buy adult tickets at the movies.
7. Being asked on dates.
8. Not being asked on dates.

Sally says that responsibility is empowering, zits can be controlled by healthy eating habits, underwear can be very cute, and dates and dances can be fun. She says algebra and the adult ticket thing suck.

MARCH 18

Sally and I used to play a game in which we'd try to decide who people we knew would be if they were characters in books. Like in *Winnie-the-Pooh,* Sally would be Kanga, because she gets fussy and motherly and gives everybody vitamin pills, and I would be Eeyore, because I'm gloomy and don't have any friends, though Sally says I'm more like Piglet, who is very likable but who worries too much.

I always thought my father would be Tigger because he was always bouncy and fun and energetic and full of things to do. But now I think he's more like Edmund, the selfish brother in *The Lion, the Witch, and the Wardrobe,* the one who didn't care what happened to anybody else as long as he got lots of enchanted Turkish delight.

My father said he was going to come visit, but now he's not going to after all.

He says Kim needs him. I don't understand why Kim has to need him right now. He's there with her all the time.

If somebody were to drag me off to the Underworld, I'd stay there and never come back, no matter how much they mooched around up above crying over me. But I wouldn't get trapped by a handful of stupid pomegranate seeds. I'd ask for a coconut-almond-fudge sundae.

## MARCH 26

Everybody is mad at me for telling the truth.

THINGS I TOLD THE TRUTH ABOUT
1. George's mother.
2. Marriage.
3. What Andrea really looks like in her red
   pants.

I told George that his mother was not a star. Dead people get buried in the ground, where they rot and turn into dust, and you never see them again, ever.

I told Sally that her life was a lie because she and my father had promised to love and cherish each other as long as they both lived and they didn't.

I told Andrea that those red pants make her rear end look really, really huge.

Everybody hates me. But I think people should face facts and tell the truth and not go around being hypocrites all the time.

APRIL 4

The Underworld is behind the upright piano.

Horace and I are spending a lot of time there because the second grade has gotten involved in the play. They are doing a snowflake dance while Demeter mopes around about me going to hell and makes everything winter. All the snowflakes wear white sweatshirts and boings with cut-out paper snowflakes that bobble around when they dance. They look like a lot of short albino beetles.

Horace says his parents lie too. When he was four, he found Bubbles, his goldfish, floating upside down in his bowl. His parents told him that Bubbles was asleep.

Later Horace found out that they flushed Bubbles down the toilet.

Andrea has given her red pants to Goodwill.

George isn't speaking to me. He thinks I'm mean.

## APRIL 10

Last night Katie Costello had a dream about getting on the school bus and then discovering that she'd forgotten to put on her clothes. She wasn't naked or anything though. She was wearing these very cute pink flannel pajamas.

THINGS I FOUND OUT TODAY ABOUT DREAMS
1. Ryan Matthews can smell things in his dreams.
2. Jason Dobbs has nightmares about spiders.
3. Ronnie Pincus always dreams in black and white. He says it's because when his mother was pregnant with him, all they had to watch was this very old black-and-white TV set.
4. Emily Harris says that when you dream about something you really want, that means it's going to come true.
5. Horace says that dreams are the products of the subconscious mind.

I had a dream too. In my dream it was one of those really perfect spring days. The sky was pale,

pale blue like forget-me-nots, and the daffodils were out all along the stone wall behind our house, dozens and dozens of them, like all these little suns, and in my dream I just knew something wonderful was about to happen. It was that Christmas-morning sort of feeling, all happy and excited, when your blood feels like it's all full of fizzy little bubbles, like ginger ale. So I came downstairs and Sally was sitting in the kitchen in her prettiest dress, the green gauzy one with the embroidery around the hem, with the sun shining all around her, and she smiled at me and said "It's going to be today, you know" and I knew she meant the something wonderful. And then there was a knock on the front door. So I went to answer it and my father was standing there, and he was smiling too, and he said "Hello, pumpkin, I've come home" and in the dream I was so happy that I didn't even care that he called me pumpkin, which I hate.

Then I woke up.

APRIL 12

Sally told me why my father needs to stay with Kim just now. Kim is having a baby. It's making her sick. My father is taking care of her.

> *feckless* (adj.) Unthinking,
> irresponsible.

That is what Andrea called my father.

Sally says that is not fair. People change, Sally says, and when you care for someone, you want them to have what they need to be happy.

I think if people are going to change, they shouldn't get married in the first place.

Also I think Sally could have tried harder to be what my father needed to be happy. She could have put on fingernail polish and stopped wearing those ratty jeans with the hole in the knee.

So much for dreams.

## APRIL 19

Horace and I spent most of the afternoon in the Underworld. Horace sat on the floor and I sat on the piano bench. While the second grade was practicing its snowflake dance, Horace explained his Theory of Ethical Lying. I am wrong about always telling the truth, Horace says. Sometimes lying is morally justified.

Also Benjamin Franklin's list is not perfect. For example, it doesn't say anything about not killing cows to make hamburgers.

Horace is a vegetarian.

WHEN LYING IS JUSTIFIED, ACCORDING TO
HORACE

1. When your grandmother knits you a stupid orange hat shaped like a jellyfish and gives it to you for your birthday and then asks you how you like it.

2. When you are helping fugitive slaves and the slave catchers ask you if there is anybody hidden under the floorboards in the living room and there is.

3. When there are spotted owls living in the trees next to your house and a hunter asks you if you've seen any owls.
4. When your mother asks you if you've done your math homework and you say yes, you have, even though you haven't, but you only do it to save her stress and worry.
5. When at the time you thought you were telling the truth but later you reconsidered and changed your mind in light of present circumstances.
6. When telling the truth would really hurt somebody's feelings.

I told Horace what I said to George about the star.

WHEN LYING IS JUSTIFIED, ACCORDING TO HORACE
7. When telling the truth would really, really upset a little five-year-old kid.

APRIL 21

GOOD PEOPLE

1. Mother Teresa

2. Martin Luther King, Jr.

3. Abraham Lincoln

4. Mahatma Gandhi

BAD PEOPLE

1. Hitler

2. Attila the Hun

3. Darth Vader

4. Me

Everybody hates me.

I wish I could just live in the Underworld forever.

APRIL 24

Sally says that when you've done something mean, you will never feel better until you apologize. So I have apologized to George and Sally and Andrea.

WHAT THEY SAID
1. Okay.
2. That's all right, sweetheart; you've been having a hard time.
3. Don't worry about it, kid. I don't know what I was thinking when I bought those damn pants.

I still don't feel better. George didn't mean it when he said okay. He wouldn't look at me and he was talking from behind his bear.

It's awful when a little kid stops liking you. George used to follow me around all the time and was always asking me to read to him and help him make raspberry Jell-O and stuff. He's really pretty cute, George. He has a sort of little pointed face like an elf and he wears these baggy little overalls.

George doesn't like the name George either.

He wants to be called Willoughby.

Willoughby is a character in George's favorite picture book, which is all about these bears who live in a cave and sleep in bunk beds and have adventures. Willoughby sleeps in the top bunk bed. He is a very short bear.

APRIL 27

Today is the anniversary of the day Sally and Jonah met. They are celebrating it. Jonah brought Sally a big bouquet of yellow roses, and they have gone out to dinner. Sally was wearing her green dress. That dress makes her skin look creamy and her eyes look really green. Jonah just kept looking at her.

Jonah was wearing a suit jacket, but even that doesn't help his belly. I don't know what Sally can be thinking. My father runs and works out at the gym. Emily Harris says my father is really hot.

Jonah isn't.


I called my father in California.

This is what he said: *Kim and Greg cannot come to the phone at this time. If you leave a message after the beep, they will return your call as soon as they can.*

**Later**

My father has returned my call. He's had a lot on his mind, he says. He's worried about Kim. She keeps throwing up. Also they hadn't expected her to get pregnant, and it's taken a lot of getting used to.

I know what Andrea would say about this, because I already heard her saying it to Sally in the kitchen.

WHAT ELSE MY FATHER SAID ON THE
TELEPHONE
1. He is going to come see me in the play.
2. He has a lot of things to talk to me about.

Maybe he wants me to come live in California with him. I could help take care of the baby.

Nobody wants me around here.

MAY 5

Sally and Jonah have decided to move in together. I knew this was going to happen. All that "We're just friends" stuff was just too good to be true.

First Sally told me privately by myself and Jonah told George. Then they both told both of us together. Jonah got very solemn and made a little speech and told me that though of course he knows he can never take the place of my real father, he hopes I'll come to regard him as a father too. The more fathers in your corner, the better, Jonah said.

Sally just hugged George. George is all excited. He is already calling Sally "Mom." He thinks we're all going to be a family and live happily ever after. He doesn't understand that we will never be a family. Families are born, not patched together.

REASONS WHY SALLY CAN'T MARRY JONAH

1. He wears socks with his sandals.
2. He sings "Puff, the Magic Dragon."
3. He likes pea soup.
4. Our house doesn't have enough room.
5. George hates me.

MAY 9

Horace says I am too stupid to appreciate my good luck. He thinks Jonah is great. According to Horace, the SAVE THE WHALES bumper stickers show that Jonah's heart is in the right place. Horace says you can tell a lot about a person by their bumper stickers.

REASONS WHY HORACE KNOWS NOTHING
ABOUT THIS
1. Horace's parents have never been divorced.

BUMPER STICKERS OF PEOPLE I KNOW

1. Ronnie Pincus's father's pickup truck has a green bumper sticker that says FUND FAMILY FARMS.

2. Jason Dobbs's father's pickup truck has a red-white-and-blue bumper sticker that says WHEN GUNS ARE CRIMINAL, ONLY CRIMINALS WILL HAVE GUNS.

3. Emily Harris's mother's car has a pink bumper sticker that says MARY KAY COSMETICS.

4. Andrea's VW Beetle has an orange bumper sticker that says A WOMAN NEEDS A MAN LIKE A FISH NEEDS A BICYCLE.

5. Katie Costello's parents' station wagon has a powder-blue bumper sticker that says WE SUPPORT NATIONAL MOTHERS OF TWINS CLUBS.

6. Ryan Matthews's mother's car has a black-and-white bumper sticker that says GRAVITY: IT'S THE LAW.

7. Sally has half of a bumper sticker that says VOTE FOR that was on the car when she bought it and she scraped off the part she didn't approve of, and a whole bumper sticker that says THE ARTS ARE NOT A LUXURY.

8. Horace Zimmerman's parents' cars have bumper stickers that say SAVE THE SPOTTED OWL, STOP GLOBAL WARMING, GET INVOLVED, PEACE BEGINS WHEN THE HUNGRY ARE FED, and ACTIONS SPEAK LOUDER THAN BUMPERS.

9. My father's convertible has a bumper sticker that says CLUB MED.

When I have a car, I want a bumper sticker like the one I saw last week in the Pelham Friendly Supermarket parking lot. It said PLEASE FORGIVE ME. I WAS RAISED BY WOLVES.

Horace says if I get a bumper sticker, it should read DON'T BELIEVE EVERYTHING YOU THINK.

Horace can be very annoying.

MAY 12

My father is not coming to the play. He can't leave Kim. She is still sick.

HOW I FEEL ABOUT THIS
1. Mad.

**MAY 14**

Sally doesn't get angry very often, which goes to show that red hair doesn't always mean a hot temper. Not that Sally's hair is orange like mine, but it's definitely reddish. A sort of copper color.

Today she got angry at me. She said that I am moping around making everybody miserable and that I am thinking only of myself.

OTHER THINGS SALLY SAID TO ME
1. Sooner or later bad things happen to everybody.
2. But we have to pull ourselves together and move on.
3. Sulking won't make the divorce go away.
4. I should be glad for my father about Kim and the baby.
5. I should be glad for her about finding Jonah.
6. Instead of deliberately making everybody feel guilty all the time.
7. And she can't stand much more of this.

So then I got angry too.

I yelled and threw a spoon.

After all, it's not like Sally got stuck in a mess. Or my father. Sally is running around with Jonah, picking out this special wallpaper that's made out of something like soybeans. My father is lying around next to a swimming pool with Kim. They're not stuck with anything. The person who is stuck is me.

THINGS I SAID TO SALLY

1. She messed up my life.
2. If anybody is selfish around here, it's her.
3. She never even asked me about Jonah moving in.
4. How come I don't ever have a say in anything?
5. Why does everybody get what they want except me?
6. And how come we didn't celebrate Purple Feathered Hat Day that she'd promised we'd celebrate together all the rest of our lives?
7. And if she were any kind of a good mother, she wouldn't act like that.

Then Sally burst into tears and ran out of the kitchen and went upstairs to her bedroom and slammed the door.

I went to my bedroom and slammed the door too.

This is all Sally's fault.

WHAT I HAVE DECIDED TO DO

1. Run away from home and live in New York City and never speak to Sally again as long as I live.

Later

I've been hating Sally for three hours.

But then it got hard to stay angry. Right at first when you get angry, it feels like you're going to stay that way forever. You want to scream and stamp and bite and smash things, and you think of all the really terrible things you could do to everybody.

But then, no matter how hard you try to hold on to being angry, the feeling just gradually starts to ooze away. I don't mean I wasn't still mad at Sally. I just stopped wanting to throw stuff at her.

Also I was hungry.

So I went downstairs and Sally was sitting at the kitchen table looking miserable and all red and puffy around the eyes.

It serves her right, I thought.

But before I could say anything, Sally looked up and said, "You're right, I should have asked you. And I feel horrible about Purple Feathered Hat Day. I wouldn't blame you if you hated me."

So I told her I didn't hate her exactly.

Then I made a piece of peanut-butter toast and Sally made a cup of tea and we had a long talk.

Sally said if it's not okay with me about Jonah and George moving in, then they won't. It's my house too, and it wouldn't be fair.

But I could tell that she really, really wanted them to.

So I said it was okay.

I guess Jonah's really not so bad.

Horace says it's not Jonah's fault he's going bald. It's because of a chromosome he inherited from his mother.

**Even Later**

After I talked to Sally, I called my father and said it was all right about him not coming to the play. And I said I was happy about the baby, and I even asked how Kim was feeling, which was really polite of me, seeing that I don't care. Sally thinks I should be nicer to people, but I'm not going to get stupid about it.

If the baby is a girl, Kim wants to name her Moonlight Sonata.

Andrea says that's the dippiest thing she's ever heard.

PEOPLE I MADE UP WITH TODAY

1. Sally.
2. My father.

PEOPLE I HAVEN'T MADE UP WITH

1. George.

**MAY 20**

I am in debt for life to geeky Horace Zimmerman. This is how it happened.

Sally and Jonah went off to pack the stuff at Jonah's house into boxes. While they were packing, I was supposed to take care of George and keep him from getting underfoot. So I took him and his bear for a walk down to the pond.

George wasn't very happy about being with me, and he wouldn't look at me, but he came along anyway. The pond is back in the woods, and there's a little path that leads to it. It's one of my favorite places, the pond. There are water lilies there and cattails and lots of googly little frogs, and the water is clear, clear green. We sat down next to the water and George wouldn't talk to me, but I could tell that he was thinking. George isn't like most little kids. He doesn't just run around and yell all the time. He really thinks about things, and sometimes you can just see him worrying and turning things over in his head.

Then he started to cry. Not sobbing or yelling like he does when he falls down and skins his knee, but tears just bubbling up and running down his cheeks without making a sound.

It was all because of his mother and that stupid thing I said about the star.

So George is crying and I feel like crying too because I've ruined everything between us by opening my big mean stupid mouth and then somebody said, "What's the matter?" and it was Horace Zimmerman with a jelly jar. He was there to collect pond water to look at under his microscope.

With anybody else I would have been embarrassed, but there's no point in front of Horace. He's already so weird.

"What's the matter?" Horace said again, and then he sat down and I told him, and he said, "Hey, George," and then he explained, which is why I am in debt for life to geeky Horace Zimmerman.

This is what he said:

Everything we're made of, Horace says, comes from stars. All the heavy elements on earth were made in an exploding star. Copper and silver and gold and things like that. They're all from supernovas. We're all cobbled together from little bits of star.

"What happens when you die?" George said, with his face in his bear.

Nobody knows exactly, is what Horace said. But all those elements we're made of drift off to become parts of other things. Like grass and roses and rabbits and clouds and diamonds and bears.

And even, after a long, long time, new stars.

So George stopped crying and thought about that for a while, and then he said, "Okay," but this time it was a good kind of "Okay." Not like before.

So I said, "I'm really sorry, George. I was mean, and I promise never to do that again." And I hugged him, and he hugged me back and things would have gotten mushy except that right then Horace fell into the pond while trying to catch a salamander.

(MORE) GOOD THINGS ABOUT HORACE
2. He is really kind.

Horace Zimmerman is in disgrace. It's all because of taking a stand against world hunger again. This time he took his stand in Act II of the play.

In Act II, I have been kidnapped. I am in the Underworld waiting for my next big scene in which (big mistake) I eat the pomegranate seeds. On stage, Demeter is crying and wailing and wearing a gray wool wig. All the other gods and goddesses are yelling at her because she hasn't bothered to take care of the crops. Everybody else is lying around on the ground, holding their stomachs and starving to death. Except the second-graders, who just did their snowflake dance.

Then Horace Zimmerman, who wasn't supposed to be doing anything yet, jumped out from behind the piano and started yelling and waving this huge poster in the air. The poster said:

**People are starving EVERYWHERE.**

**STOP WORLD HUNGER!**

**SIGN MY PETITION IN THE LOBBY.**

Ms. Bentley was furious at Horace for ruining the play. She started yelling, "Horace Zimmerman, sit down this instant!" from backstage. But she couldn't get at him because she was trapped by thirty second-grade snowflakes.

"Sit down, kid!" somebody bellowed from the audience. It was Emily Harris's father.

Everybody was muttering and looking sideways at Horace Zimmerman's parents, who have raised such an awful son, and Horace Zimmerman's parents were looking resigned. They're used to Horace.

A couple of people started booing.

Horace was still yelling about stopping world hunger and about acting locally but thinking globally, and about everyone being able to make a difference, but you could tell he was starting to get upset because taking a stand wasn't working out the way he had expected. And I am in debt to Horace Zimmerman for life. So I crawled out from behind the piano and stood up next to him in my pillowcase and my stupid wreath of toilet-paper flowers and started yelling about stopping world hunger too.

And then Jonah, who was sitting right in the front with Sally and George, stood up and started shouting, "Bravo!" Jonah is fat and going bald and his shirttail was hanging out, and he was really loud. The first thing I thought was that my father would never make a fool of himself in public like that. And then Horace started grinning, and all of a sudden I was really glad that Jonah would. In a weird kind of way, Horace and Jonah are a lot alike. Neither of them cares how dumb he looks as long as he's doing what he thinks is right.

Then Sally and George stood up too, and George started jumping up and down and yelling, "Horace! Horace! Sarah! Sarah!" and waving his bear.

Then Horace Zimmerman's parents stood up, and then Ronnie Pincus's parents stood up because, having a family farm, they are sensitive about crop failures. So Ronnie Pincus, who was being Zeus, came down from Olympus, which was the janitor's stepladder, and started waving his cardboard thunderbolt and yelling with us. And then Emily Harris came over, wearing her pillowcase and a lot of gold hair ribbons to show that she was Aphrodite, and started yelling too, which is something I would never have expected in a million years.

Then Ms. Zebrowski stood up.

Pretty soon people were standing up all over the place.

Then Ms. Bentley finally untangled herself from the snowflakes and things started quieting down, but before a single word came out of her mouth, Jonah came bounding up on the stage in his dippy shirt with the zebras on it and shook her hand and congratulated her on the creativity of her approach and the inspiring attitude of her students, so she said "Thank you" instead of all the things she'd been about to say, and then everybody clapped.

We never finished the play.

Practically everybody signed Horace's petition, except Emily Harris's parents, who are mad at him. They wanted to see Emily make her big entrance with a laundry basket full of plastic fruit.

WHAT PEOPLE SAID TO HORACE AFTERWARD

1. Congratulations, young man.
2. Totally awesome.
3. You jerk.
4. I'll see you in my office on Monday.

MAY 25

My father says he's really sorry he missed the play. He also says he's proud of me. Sally must have told him what happened.

He thinks that Jonah sounds like a great guy and that Horace is probably right about bumper stickers. The night he met Kim, he says, she was wearing a SAVE THE RAIN FOREST T-shirt. (And a miniskirt the size of a postage stamp, says Andrea.) Still, anyone who thinks about the rain forest, says Horace, can't be all bad.

My father hopes Kim and I will learn to love each other like sisters someday, since Kim isn't old enough to be my mother.

I said I'd think about it.

## JUNE 13

Today is my birthday. I have become a teenager.

Sally gave me a dress in a sort of turquoise-y color that actually makes my orange hair look sort of nice, and a set of removable tattoos, and a purple feathered hat, a really goony one with ostrich plumes. There was a dinner invitation taped to it.

Jonah gave me an astronomy book.

George gave me a butterfly made out of a paper plate that he made in kindergarten.

Horace Zimmerman made a donation in my name to the Save the Spotted Owl Foundation.

For dinner Sally made me a carrot cake with cream-cheese frosting, because that's my favorite, with thirteen candles on it, and we drank toasts to many happy returns in ginger ale. Then everybody sang, and George made me wear this birthday crown that he and Jonah made out of construction paper and aluminum foil.

George and Jonah have moved in with us.

What used to be the guest bedroom is now George's bedroom. Sally painted it yellow, which is his favorite color, and made curtains with a pattern of bears.

Sally and Jonah are in the big bedroom that used to be hers and my father's. They've moved the furniture in the study around so that there's room for Jonah's desk.

Sally and Jonah are really happy. Anyone can see it. They go around looking all lit up inside. When they get married, sometime this summer, I am going to be the maid of honor. George is going to be the flower boy, and Horace Zimmerman is going to play "We Shall Overcome" and "Puff, the Magic Dragon" on the violin.

Jonah says "We Shall Overcome" is a cherished song from the days of his distant youth, but I think there's more to it than that. I think it's a song for all of us in our family because we've all had to overcome stuff and move on.

"Puff, the Magic Dragon" is for George.

George thinks there's an invisible dragon living in the woods behind our house. He says that he knows it's there because when he puts out food, the dragon comes and eats it.

I think it's raccoons, but I'm not going to say so.

Today was the last day of school. Everybody talked about what they are going to do over the summer.

Here is what they said:

1. Emily Harris is going to interpretive-dance camp.
2. Ronnie Pincus is helping his father cut hay.
3. Jason Dobbs is going to the stock-car races.
4. Ryan Matthews is going to the Smithsonian Museum.
5. Katie Costello is babysitting for her three-year-old twin sisters.
6. Horace Zimmerman is making a stand against world poverty.

Everybody except Jason promised to help Horace make his stand, even Emily Harris, whose parents do not exactly approve of their daughter's consciousness being raised, but it's too late now. I guess it isn't Emily's fault that she's blond.

Even if we just make a little difference, Horace says, that's still something. And if everybody makes a little difference, sooner or later all those little bits add up.

I've been thinking lately about my New Year's resolutions. The year is half over and none of them have come to anything, not even the one about dyeing my horrible hair. Maybe it's just as well. Anyway, I wouldn't make the same resolutions now. Everything has changed. Nobody was exactly like I thought they were, and nothing turned out the way I thought it would.

Back in January I felt like my life was over and nothing would ever be happy again. Now I think I was full of crap. Sally says I'm growing up. Horace thinks I'm developing a political conscience. Jonah says time has a way of healing all kinds of wounds. George thinks it all has something to do with stars and bears.

I'm not sure. But for right now, I'm hoping for the best, just like Ms. Zebrowski said.

OTHER THINGS I'VE LEARNED THIS YEAR SO FAR
1. It's what you are, not what you look like, that's important.
2. People can make a difference.

3. Things that fall apart have a way of coming back together again.
4. We're all made of little bits of stars.

5. Even Kim.

ACKNOWLEDGMENTS

Many thanks to all who helped in the making of this book, among them Joshua Rupp, who supported Sarah's story every step of the way; Cynthia Platt, my patient editor, who defended Emily Harris; Charlotte Platt-Miller, who generously shared her mother during her very first months on earth; and all the talented and wonderful people at Candlewick who make books possible.

**Rebecca Rupp,** a versatile and productive writer, is the author of nonfiction articles for many national magazines on topics ranging from the history of blue jeans to the science of ice cream. She is the author of several novels for children, including *The Dragon of Lonely Island* and *The Return of the Dragon, The Waterstone,* and *Journey to the Blue Moon: In Which Time Is Lost and Then Found Again.* A seasoned practitioner of homeschooling, she has written several books on the subject, including *The Complete Home Learning Sourcebook.* Another of her titles, *Everything You Never Learned About Birds,* is an informative resource full of hands-on science projects and a part of the Everything You Never Learned series, popular with both educators and parents. Her books for adults include *Committed to Memory: How We Remember and Why We Forget.* Rebecca Rupp lives in Vermont with her family.